ON FICTION

Janet Kauffman

FIVE ON FICTION

BURNING DECK
PROVIDENCE 2004

Some of these texts have appeared in *13th Moon,*
Caliban, The Colorado Review, Controlled Burn, Sulfur.

ISBN 1-886224-73-0 original paperback
ISBN 1-886224-74-9 original paperback, signed edition

CONTENTS

On Eliminating Characters from Fiction

1.

If you don't say the name of a person, a good many
things are possible in a sentence, and even in a landscape
without margins or verifiable boundaries. It is possible
to turn a corner and encounter a large machine lifting
trees out of the ground. You can read the lettering on the
metal, letters and numbers that are a code name for the
machine, but it is certainly not the name of a person.
Heaps of trees in full leaf may be stacked in the middle
of the road. It is possible to see the beginnings of flames
among the branches, and if you wait long enough, not
very long actually, turn slightly to the side, and still not
saying the name of a person, you can walk through the
fire and into the house it's become.

2.

It's akin to making a hat from sticks. The handwork and gluing are not at all sweatshopped. Not jetted or crashed into wetlands, not magically rising up out of it whole and crowned. You can count the prepositions, cross-fingered, coming up from to out of, especially. And it is a cityscape here. Swept. There's plenty of sand for the froth of some sea.

8.

Okay, explain how many celebrations it takes to call
them off and quit firing k-k-k-k-k-k-k into clouds,
fireworks falling onto cottonwoods where they spit
jewelry and metal chunks of Pontiacs, the whole river
valley flipped to an attic with clothing on dummies,
strings of paper lights burning; how many long naps with
sun-block and hand-held missile launchers, before night
and nothing else falls, and time (paying no attention to
all the fucking goodbyes) passes.

4.

And the story that stops with somebody saying fare-thee-well to somebody must be false. Even if there's scenery in the fade-out. A dead tree, say. Even if the kid says something like, "I'll get those chives chopped now, Mother." Even if he says, "Bring me my goose gun." He goes inside, and in the middle of chive-chopping, or later, maybe stories later, fork in his hand, he's opening his mouth.

5.

In their cells, in their cells, they invent vocabularies
ready-to-go. They don't have paint or soldering tools,
but they do have the diehard mentality. They don't scrub
up. Their spirits have so completely filled them out, gone
right past the skin, detached, that these are the things
cited, proof on paper of whatever's lost or found, which
is why, even if we have lamps, good light, we can't know
by reading who is who.

6.

Debris, homespun, flim-flamming with shrouds, cast-offs, that is the handwork of what's-her-name in her shift, her hair woven to ladders. It is the paradox of her escape, she climbs down, she cuts her hair, more flotsam to figure out. She is gone, gone, a nervy babe, like a one-time flier, flimsy above the globe and going down. Oh, those are the syllables she calls out, oh, oh.

7.

On its own, narrative goes to nature. His tongue between her toes, or hers his, they roll in a tire, say, one way and another, steel-belted, hot as the highway, it's Utah anyhow, the salt flats, fast with their fingers between their thighs. They don't know which way they'll roll next, whoever's story it is. Is this day the equinox? They're spun, they shut their eyes to cut out confusion, and hollows open up behind their knees and, see, it's Salt Lake between them. They lick whatever they can, and slow. It's not true, but people say it: this is the ocean that used to be.

8.

Recall the trees, their ex-foliage — in French, a construction more tactile. In fiction, the mouth is the place of trees, whole: root, trunk, limb, leaf, seed, node, scar, tooth, tip, pit, lobe.

9.

It's raining, and yes, somewhere the avalanches strip stones from the cliff, wing-scrapes. There is so much motion the sow-bugs roll downhill, and then the artillery opens up and shells hit the three-story apartment buildings at 16 Ferdinand Place and the windows flare. They have exploded now. The gnats called phantom gnats with fringed antennae as large as wings, the ones walking the corners of the glass, they are in the air now, and you've flown here, your baggage is so light.

10.

They're sleeping in a row, labeled, you can look, it's not like tags on their toes, but they've got a line or two over their heads, bookish, like poets, maybe they are poets, side by side, you can call up their files at the windows. They've been asleep, arranged in some fashion, and now we're here messing up the sheets, good god, air the place out, open another door. Even your mother says, there's more than scenery out there. You can look both ways, and then another, the first disturbance is the most disturbing, and after that you can read the books with the bad titles, and make love this way, one leg over the shoulder.

On Plot, as Ground

1.

Bleed it, run it over, past the margin or whatever edge of the thing hedges the page, garden, sheet, highway, screen. There's the body, too, and when the format or the shoulder cuts off, drops off, and it's not possible to go over and under the asphalt or onto the reverse of the surface, moebius-stripped, or inside the skin, and the eye is exposed to the same plane and cut of things, well, the mind does for the mind what it can. A blur and flux and more of the same until somebody says, stop! And then bleed that, run it over, a surface a place a form a fake a violence a turn to it and from it.

2.

One thing a kid calls music crosses the street. It is not bird song, but fish or mouth shapes flying, hammered, cast brass or tin chimes on the wood porch of a boarded house, not her house. And no one walks in or walks out, but the sound flies, and it is the girl's jangling teeth, there with her carved jaw on the sand, not one room or ceiling for her across a whole desert, and she lies where the other end of the wind rattles through, at her mother's feet.

2.

It would be better, when it matters most, to see in secret, and read, to look at a canvas with blue and black paints on it, with its various songs and assaults and logics, alone, or with one other person, two at the most, and lie around looking at words wherever they lie, too, or to circulate anything like art like contraband so that possession is moral complicity, a wrestling, right to the ground.

4.

As economical postlude, whack a peaky mountain down. Something along the line of rubble, pebbled, and here are enough ringable stones for all the pinkie fingers you can count. Ringmasters, quite a bunch, call in the clean-up crews — clowns they've never been happy with, with brooms, horns, blowers, scrubbers, the racket of room-size polishers. And then they raise a stink, it's work work, and what the hell happened, they want to know, to the pie-faced high-topped comical?

5.

Tobacco sizing boxes are real things, enclosed steps, six up or six down, depending how you look at them. Right justified. You can still read the leaves now and then, and in the tobacco-stripping room in November, anybody says anything. The dry leaves are sized, baled, it's hand-work all the way, and on the table, the radio plays, too. As good as an open field, what we've got is dust, and, go ahead, call it your working proof of life elsewhere, of the relativity of time and this space, of fiction as what any body says.

6.

Pass Monsieur Pasha, make it a dish from the past, with heft, an excess of sauce, European and entrepreneurial, sleek in velvets and patent leather, all sorts of imports, indisputable, entirely seigniorial, smooth in its etymologies, the Madeira, the port, the heap of it, haul it along like a pyramid or a davenport. Eat in the living room. Maybe a kid'll deliver it. Maybe the women'll clean up.

7.

It's only one thing, their cry, but profligate, the high romance of four or maybe more fingers at play, soloing Paganini. Hell, it's not easy when you're good to have fun. But when you're expert, the excess — hear that? They used to say it was siren-song, off the water, and what else do women have to do out there but call like that. They've been at it all their lives. They know there's no end to pleasure. That's what they have to say. No wonder they lounge around, unpaid like you and me, who kick it up with the fishes, and open our eyes, and cry out again.

8.

The number of wing-feathers (f) it takes to circum-
navigate a given planet (x) is directly proportional to
the number of armed men (m) it takes to subjugate half
the population of that world ($1/2\ p$ of x), so that most
species and certainly all the poor, adept in mathematics
from perpetual practice, prefer either flocks of relaying
flocks or those infamous contraptions like Icarus' that
gum together random collections of pin feathers,
secondaries, down, and plumes, rather than air to air
missiles, calculated spans of selected lightweight
alloys, riveted, polished like teeth.

9.

Consider the Catholic boy brain mazes, the dark and depth of God, who ditched them, back there somewhere, predecessor, and now they're on their own, Hansels in the woods, lederhosen in good shape. Although it's not their legs they care for, not their arms they swing through the speckle shade places, not anybody else's body they hand-hold, or care-take in the end. No, here, sit here at all the machinery, they've got the codes, it's a revelation, the goodly heaps of God's waste at each of the grid's embroidered nodes, they'll go clean to the core — where roots root, they say, and rot rots.

10.

So this is the end of holding the book like a head, there are so many hairs on his head, one after another. It's the end of holding the book like a fish, fingered, a limb, all of his letters, the print thick as the lawn. She is reading the book barefoot, reading the book, its letters, not his letters, and touching them with her fingers. The book falls on her wrists where the skin is thin and soft. The book is bound, she can feel that on her wrists, the binding. She is slung in the canvas sling chair. The book slips on her belly, slides between her legs. Oh, this is a very good book.

On Dialogue, Words That Come Out of the Mouth

1.

What about Angela, with a name like that, what can she say? She crosses the street whenever she wants and doesn't look over her shoulder. She wears her lapel pins for good works, she is almost metallic, shoe to hat. Her medals hang from her ears. She insists on an A, her athletic letter. She knows that whatever stars or stripes she wears, somebody will say it's too much, and it is, she is making sounds, she is breathing the smell of sex out of her mouth.

2.

She knows how talk goes, under, between, across,
buried, uprooted, dredged, hauled, maneuvered, sliced,
snagged, catapulted, pinioned, rendered, masked,
launched, labored, obliterated, hacked, hewn, harbored,
boomeranged, laid waste.

2.

It's real estate, hey, watch the ducks on the water,
somebody says. Tanks and gold finches the same thing,
knocked from chartreuse, the shock of one blink, one
more, they're butter lemon paint applied by knife.
Somebody's got the art kit. It's breakfast time, too, time
to lick the spoons, and say, gimme the cash, or say, so
what's been carved up out there now?

4.

You can't say whether weather does this damage, and more, and more. The dry lake. The bulldozed slopes. We've said too much. Look at the words. Still more.

It is only one side, but she's cut and bleeding on the foot, on the calf lengthwise and crosswise, look, on the knee as well, the thigh. She is not cut on the belly or on the breast. She is cut on the shoulder and on the forearm, she is cut on the wrist. And children on the sidewalk back away, mouths O O, and grown men step off the curb and cross over the street, they won't grab that one by the arm. You can see how freely she walks from here to there, spared, exposed, what we call fear gone out of her, whole; everything else about her here.

B.

Angelo's a hero here for that o at the end, the circle of his uncatalogued arms, his long-distance legs, he flies low, evades radar, and on the front porch says something unclear, hello, to Angelina maybe it is, there's nothing to them but air-lifted bodies, which they have named outright, and spell out now. They are nowhere near dead, as he begins the roundabout fingering of her lips, around in her mouths, and she circles him, o Angelo, arms and legs, too, unnumbed. They laugh at the cheer he gives when she comes, o Angelo. She refuses to say out loud, o God.

7.

It was said words came out of her mouth you could read. She was bearded sometimes with words. Unless the wind stripped them off. She was breathless then, conversant with vegetation, the monosyllabic reeds in particular.

8.

Maybe it's the Taj Mahal, or a pagoda, that swan or pontoon boat or head-on-wheels, the girl says. If you don't blink now, you'll never know.

9.

Backwards blowing from the East, that's not the usual way things go. Look at the gray clouds, scrim torn and dangled, you can touch them. And nobody minds for a change, walking is pool-like, pond paddling. The striated muscles take it slow, buoyant from whatever air flows by. Even old men, with the sparest flesh on long bones, stride along the marsh. They see herons flying, and the herons' eyes meet their eyes. They take in the sights, which are the lowering dark clouds, before their bodies lift and they disappear head-first, calling back in a heron's croak: Black! Blue!

10.

Too much agreeable quiet-speaking, sure, sure, it wipes you out. I bet that's why you're checking the map, you get the idea. Who cares where we are, as long as there's good cause to complain, it's about time, and somebody new to keep an eye on, water in the vicinity. Pavement so we don't forget which planet we're on. Nerves on edge, good, that's something to talk about. Who's mad now, that guy in the cap? Ask what he's done this time, you know it means trouble. He's bought the farm, the town, he's bought Seattle, he likes the needle, and thinks it's pretty, so keep up the racket, what have you got to lose. There's a measurable quantity of air left. You saw the woman with the black skirt dyed to match her hair, you know the logic, so look around. Here's a couple of trees we can travel through.

On the Transportation
of Background to Foreground

1.

Remember. Indoors, the outgoing door opens in. As a usual thing. Outdoors, the ingoing door opens out. And in a house of many doors, such as the city, the distinction, inside to out, may be difficult, an habitual mystery, what with the trees and jungle paraphernalia of tattoo shops and the concrete bedding and awned walkways under the air. Guess where you are. It is impossible to be a stranger to the climates of seven continents. And others. There are several others. The forearm registers low-lying air, off the chocolate pecan tub; and the various underground weathers rise, usually visibly, against the knee, the thigh. There is the underarm atmosphere, too — dank, hair sweet. Temperature and steam and aroma, these ephemera, forewarn the way advertising forewarns: by assertion, mild haste, dispersal. It slips by. But if you open a door, out or in, to look at an advertisement, that's another story. If you open a door, flat on the ground, to look at a subway, a grotto, that's another story, too. Consider the number of doors. It is morning in Detroit. You can open a door and see sixteen bolts of hand-woven purple fabric. You can open a door and see the wooden step and the marigolds. You can open a door and see a woman pull at her own nipples. It is mid-day. You can see the man in the green hat on the sidewalk. You can see brickwork. The sky is there, plain as a cake. The blue ceiling. The blue floor. The blue door.

2.

It's better for the camera to fall back and catch sky, a field like a line, not much beyond that, to show there's ground someplace, and gravity, a minor accounting of it. Or climb, go aerial, show us far-gone. Eyes turn up, sun-drawn, and something shifts, the nerves defining to infinite focus where weight works no more as measure. Whatever weather is here or there hits and saturates eyeballs, the camera's lens; collision is no accident.

2.

It was the leaf roofs that lifted and parted and flew upwards in spirals like hair cut as a gift for the woman who lived on the thirteenth floor, who reached out her window and caught these things in her arms before night fell.

4.

Walk around, the attraction in the Midwest is the
horizontal. It ought to be advertised. Make your bed
here, lie down. Even the low hills recline, decline, into
good foam ticking, cotton batting, dirt, straw, down.
Look at your feet, the toes up-turned. Where are your
hands? Behind your head. Or turn on the side, and
there's somebody else, hair on the head, on the blades
of the shoulders. You can comb the body with your
fingertips, roll him over, roll her, he's not sleeping and
neither is she. Comb the belly, take the penis between
your hands, lick your hands and let the palms swim.
There are plenty of holes for water, and whatever grows
grows out of clay, or sand, or the hand.

5.

If the bicycle is painted blue and disappears skyward outside Kalamazoo, it's no different, as far as that goes, from the bicycle painted brown that disappears ground-ward in southern India. And then you can imagine all the black-painted ones missing at dawn, and the orange ones pulled into volcanic areas or cheap sunsets. Notice how world-wide, a-top foot-propelled machinery, because of the easy-goingness of it, bodies weave in and out. In and out of *abattoirs*, concrete squares, the over-hangs of edifices and beaded doors, the smooth cuts across gravel, or through the iridescent waste in gutters. Nothing is not camouflaged. Notice how many things fly and evaporate and cannot choose appropriate times to plummet, we're past that, like satellites, out-dated, or dipper birds with wire feet, detached from nests, those streaks of color down and dirty in leaves.

6.

It doesn't take much in the way of angular shots to see
that the territories of animals, ours, are drawn in with
sails, planks, high-rises, poles, slabs, rock faces, bricks,
sheathing, siding, and how can we climb the cliffwalls to
roofs where whatever our two or four feet walk on is
ground and whatever our feet or hands hold is sky?

7.

Between the opera and the Mars game, how much empty space is there for a woman to traverse, without kits and oxygen. It could be atomic space, or cellular, the gaps nerve to nerve, really reckless. There are a number of feet of hammered floor, that's for sure, or half a block, or two mile circuits to town, three hours to whichever lake, and then to the edge of its water. Or there's the slow flight in childbirth, low along the islands of Japan, a long labor, all morning behind the eye, companion to leaf-wing butterflies, the bluest ones, approaching sun-lit inlets, ascending volcanic slopes, more and more blue between the gingko leaves in green upland gardens.

8.

Now that magic with its verifiable mayhem has flown
the coop — lost the coup, as the insiders say — it's no
surprise that a couple of Rhode Island Red hens collaborate
on architectural designs for the roofs over their heads,
Mansard or hip-roof, cathedral, insisting on skylights,
the better to manage their escapes nightly, into remote
star-places where they crow unnaturally and roll eggs
into whirlwinds seen as mist and swamp light, or pale
yolks adrift.

9.

The water table, there it is, although there is no fire floor or earth bed, not yet. Here's an air mattress. Won't you lie down? The water table lies, or stands, under the field, and it can be a surprise how close to the surface the table (never set, it's heaped) is buried, sometimes a plow-blade's depth. The metal scrapes water and the tractor sways on floating ground where crayfish have built up gray chunk chimneys. Apartments are mortared, cellars sink and fill with duckweed and water plantain. Are you rested? How long did you sleep? You can put your elbows on the table. It is floral and amoral and porous to the elements, the touch of everything.

10.

Out of the trees, from overhead, those multi-colored embroiled branches, and also from under the trunk's shade, rises and settles all the see-through-it air you can imagine, and it is darker than the air at the back of the mouth, but it swirls like that, intimate, the privacy of a global thing. It is ours, the same as dust, its palm-size touch, and the clasp in the throat is an aching, a moan, the sound of a cough, and here is the smoothing out of a withering, and the withering itself, and paper folding back, the collapse, the drench of sweat, another press of leaves.

On Action,
One Word after Another

1.

It's calm, and the slowest doves angle up from the road
onto wires, slow rises. Everything stalls, and they're safe,
it's a sort of safety, half-lidded, a lullabye before the tires
of cars and kids who aim to throw these things off. The
doves are gray, so gray one boy thinks they'll disappear
anyway into weeds, the plain space opposite sky. He's
been there and no one missed him.

2.

The skeleton truck pulled up, jammed, they could drive and walk like anybody else, and one of them at the front door held the key to the door between bone fingers. We recognized the key, its three chiseled teeth, that's how plain the situation was, and was before, and after.

9.

Dead wood burns, it passes the time, good for wood. No outlineable shapes hold up in fire, not tongues, hands, or fingers, not lips or belly, none of that. The refusals of metaphor, at least a few, are dead certainties, as consoling as, alternatively, the animations of cliché: honeymoon, for instance — *lune de miel* — such a shape, full or crescent, the hive emptied out all over it, fingers in it, flower-work, feet flying pollen, and then, now, the lovers' feet, and then, too, the sweet hands, fingers, tongues on each other's bodies, the niches of honey, excess, sun, night, flower, dream, it's all there. We might as well be on the moon, where nothing burns.

4.

Sixteen, no fifteen, children are lined up against the garden wall, one child is out-standing, rage in hand — see? — that thing in hand? One is counting, one won't, the handy one farmed out. One says, me, too. The next buckles her shoe, fear afoot, one or two's crayon boots are scrawled by the garden wall. One bows, one hangs low, one sings lowly lowly lowly. One and another shoot the breeze, and that takes two more. They're sick of the garden, they say, and won't cry.

5.

Here you can read the real end of all things. Two barns on the white horizon drop to nothing. A fog rises in the house, flows slow out the refrigerator door, and then a roiling blast-force wind, transparent, silent, hits and cracks the plaster, and the firemen out there sling hoses with no water at the power plant before all the concrete walls split apart, and like any day, there's nothing to do but work, or walk someplace; so you pick up a pencil, a pear, something for each hand for no reason.

6.

It's always March, when talk not logic flies in the face of things. There's ice on the driveway. How is it there with you? Ice crazes when geese walk. They live in the field, the garden, the drive. They stand on the asphalt slope, they slide, and they hold those gray wings wide. These are escapades, nobody flies.

7.

Suppose the woman behind the hat, that straw hat with the rip through the brim, turned around without warning and, looking at nobody, tore it off and tore it in half as best she could and threw it down. And took her shirt with the blue glass buttons, and ripped it open, and threw that down, too, over the pieces of the hat. And drew up her skirt and pulled at its blue fabric, with some difficulty, but she kept at it until the skirt split to the waist, and then the button at the waistband was no problem. After that she gripped the legholes of her underpants and ripped those apart, the seam at the elasticized waist snapping at the stitching, and since she was not wearing shoes, that was it. She could turn around, and step off, whichever way she'd intended to begin with. And don't let anybody walk up now and say there's a simple explanation, or a complicated one either.

8.

You said you skipped the Atlantic and came down hard in the field — *downtrodden,* you said, but aren't the words *uplifted, ditched*? Your legs shone silver from streetdust, and the blood on your face, from your left forearm, might have cooled someone not dreaming, but so few, you said, are not dreaming. It is terrible how you refuse refreshment, and speak too fast in all those languages. You will not take the extra steps to the woods, but what worse collapse could there be in shade? Before you go back, at least comb your hair and wash your arms in the River Raisin, where it falls over three green rocks. There is jewelweed there, related to touch-me-not, but you could.

9.

She's the one who sits on the edge of the windowsill and calls down: you forgot your underwear. Or more likely, she asks, because she likes the drum of the words in her head: what will you do when the doom is done? Or sometimes, she says, because it's the truth: you're the one in the uniform, the one I pulled down from the podium and kissed, the one who finally laughed before the trees fell and the program ended.

10.

They are sticks and stones, wrapped, and in your arms, you drop off the decorations, there are downfalls of veils and heat-pressed white plastic flowers and toweling and rags, mostly rags. You have littered the ocean, you lift them and fly them and lay them out, broken things strewn after storm; and although there has been no storm, and no one has any memory of storm, we have the words for it now.

This book was designed and computer typeset in 10 pt. Palatino by Rosmarie Waldrop, with titles in Benquiat Frisky and Zapf Chancery initials. Printed on 55 lb. Writers' Natural (an acid-free paper), smyth-sewn and glued into paper covers by McNaughton & Gunn in Saline, Michigan. The cover is by Keith Waldrop. There are 1000 copies, of which 50 are numbered and signed by the author.

Walter Abish, *99: The New Meaning*
Tom Ahern, *The Capture of Trieste*
Paul Auster, *Why Write?* [o.p.]
Alison Bundy, *DunceCap*
Marcel Cohen, *The Peacock Emperor Moth*
    [translated from the French by Cid Corman]
Norma Cole [editor/translator], *Crosscut Universe:*
    Writing on Writing from France:
    Anne-Marie Albiach, Joe Bousquet, Danielle Collobert,
    Edith Dahan, Jean Daive, André du Bouchet, Dominique
    Fourcade, Liliane Giraudon, Joseph Guglielmi, Emmanuel
    Hocquard, Roger Laporte, Roger Lewinter, Raquel,
    Mitsou Ronat, Jacques Roubaud, Agnes Rouzier, Claude
    Royet-Journoud
Robert Coover, *The Grand Hotels (of Joseph Cornell)*
Barbara Einzig, *Life Moves Outside*
Ludwig Harig, *The Trip to Bordeaux*
    [translated from the German by Susan Bernofsky]
John Hawkes, *Innocence in Extremis*
Janet Kauffman, *Five on Fiction*
Elizabeth MacKiernan, *Ancestors Maybe*
Friederike Mayröcker, *Heiligenanstalt*
    [translated from the German by Rosmarie Waldrop]

Lissa McLaughlin, *Troubled by His Complexion*

—, *Seeing the Multitudes Delayed*

Pascal Quignard, *On Wooden Tablets: Apronenia Avitia*
    [translated from the French by Bruce X]

Ilma Rakusa, *Steppe*
    [translated from the German by Solveig Emerson]

Gail Sher, *Broke Aide*

Ron Silliman, *Paradise* [o.p.]

Jane Unrue, *The House*

Dallas Wiebe, *The Transparent Eye-Ball* [o.p.]

—, *Going to the Mountain*

—, *Skyblue's Essays*

—, *The Vox Populi Street Stories*